JACKSON SQUARE

A few steps from the Mississippi River, Jackson Square was part of New Orleans' design when the city was laid out in 1721. Originally a military parade ground, the square was later named for Andrew Jackson, hero of the Battle of New Orleans in the war of 1812. Jackson Square is surrounded by historic buildings, including the Cabildo, where the Louisiana Purchase was signed, and St. Louis Cathedral. Today Jackson Square is a favorite gathering spot for tourists, who are entertained by artists, musicians, clowns, mimes, and other street performers.

THE FRENCH QUARTER

When the French colonists began to build New Orleans in the 1720s, they made a central square — now called Jackson Square — with streets laid around it in a grid pattern. Two fires almost destroyed the city in 1788 and in 1794, during the time when Spain ruled the Louisiana territory. So, although this old section is called the French Quarter, its architecture reflects the tastes of the Spanish who rebuilt it after the fires. The French Quarter today looks much as it did in the 1800s, with its colonial period buildings, quiet courtyards, and iron balconies, called galleries, overlooking narrow streets.

GUMBO

The hero of *Gumbo Goes Downtown* is named after one of the most famous dishes of Louisiana. Gumbo is a rich, spicy stew made with shrimp, crabs, oysters, chicken, ham, or even rabbit or squirrel. It is usually seasoned with thyme, bay leaf, chilies, and cayenne pepper and is thickened with okra or with filé, a powder made from sassafras leaves.

CATAHOULA HOUND

Also called the Catahoula Leopard Dog, the Cat was named the official state dog of Louisiana in 1979. The Catahoula breed is believed to be a cross between a type of dog raised by Native Americans of the Catahoula Lakes region of the state and war dogs brought by the Spanish to Louisiana in the sixteenth century.

Catahoula Hounds have a short — usually spotted — coat and webbed feet. Their eyes may be brown, green, or white (called glass eyes). Catahoula Hounds are good hunting dogs and loyal pets, and because they are usually unfriendly to strangers they make excellent guard dogs.

ST. CHARLES STREETCAR

The St. Charles Avenue streetcar line is a major tourist attraction and an important means of transportation for the citizens of New Orleans. The streetcar runs from Canal Street, clanging up St. Charles Avenue, then turning right onto Carrollton Avenue. At the end of the line, the driver walks to the other end of the car, flipping the backs of the mahogany seats, and heads back downtown. The streetcar moves along on two rails and is powered by an overhead electrical line. The St. Charles line claims to be the oldest continuously-operated streetcar system in the world.

Gumbo Goes Downtown

Written by **Carol Talley**

Illustrated by **Itoko Maeno**

MarshMedia, Kansas City, Missouri

First Printing 1993, Second Printing 2000, Third Printing 2002,
Fourth Printing 2004, Fifth Printing 2010, Sixth Printing 2012

Published by **MARSH**media

P. O. Box 8082
Shawnee Mission, KS 66208

Library of Congress Cataloging-in-Publication Data
Talley, Carol.
 Gumbo goes downtown / written by Carol Talley; illustrated by Itoko Maeno.
  p.   cm.
 Summary: Unable to scare anybody, Gumbo the watchdog runs away to the
French Quarter of New Orleans in search of a new identity.
  ISBN 978-1-55942-042-6
  1. Dogs—Juvenile fiction. [1. Dogs—Fiction. 2. Runaways—Fiction.
3. Identity—Fiction. 4. New Orleans (La.)—Fiction] I. Maeno, Itoko, ill. II. Title.
PZ10.3.T1382Gu 1993   93-3551
[E]—dc20

2012 layout revision by Elizabeth Brewer

Printed in U.S.A.

To My Sister Linda C.T.
To My Sisters Nobue and Motoko I.M.

Special thanks to Charles Hammer,
Elizabeth Happy, and Theodore Otteson, to Atom — the model
for Gumbo — and his owner Margaret Dodd, to Tapioca — the model for
the Cat — and her owner Katie Jacobs,
and to a mutt called Sparky.

My name is Gumbo, and I live in New Orleans, Louisiana, in a shotgun house right on the St. Charles streetcar line. It's called a shotgun house because you can stand in the front door and shoot your shotgun out the back door without any walls getting in the way.

Around my house is a chain-link fence, and on the fence is a sign: BEWARE OF DOG.

That's me, Gumbo.

I live with Gus. Gus is swell.
He takes me on walks.

He brushes my coat.

He scratches my belly and my back and my ears.
I have my own dish and my own bed. Gus means a lot
to me, and I mean a lot to Gus. I didn't always know that.

One day last October, I was standing watch on the front step when a girl in a polka dot dress poked her chubby fingers through the fence. I knew what she was after.

"Can't you read?" I barked, ripping up and down the yard. "Beware of dog! That's me!"

"Hello, Gumbo," she said, snapping off one of Gus's Miss All-American Beauty roses.

"That does it! That does it!" I barked. "You've had it now! You worthless dog biscuit!"

She just sashayed her polka dots on down the sidewalk, and I stood there feeling like a big nobody. What good is a watchdog if he can't scare anybody?

I was still asking myself that question the next morning when the postman walked right past my sign and through the gate.

"Can't you hear me?" I shouted, barking to raise the dead. "Pay attention to me!" He dropped a Piggly Wiggly circular into the mailbox, patted me on the head, and walked back out the gate.

But the gate didn't catch! It swung open like an invitation.

The next thing I knew, I was standing on the streetcar tracks looking down them to where they disappeared in a point. Those tracks looked like an opportunity to go someplace else, to be somebody else, to be SOMEBODY.

So I followed them — past the shotgun houses with their chain-link fences, past the old mansions with their wrought iron fences, all the way to the end of the line.

That's where I saw the dancing dog.

By the time I made it
across Canal Street, quite a crowd
had gathered. That dog was a marvel.
He danced on his hind legs. He danced on
his front legs. He danced on *one* leg!

He was in the middle of a backward flip when I caught his eye. "Bon jour,"
he barked, upside down. He went into a forward double somersault.
"Welcome —" Over he went. "— to the French Quarter." And he landed
right beside me.

Pompon — that was his name — was just the kind of accomplished canine
I had hoped to meet on my travels. I told him so, and before I knew it we were
sauntering down Royal Street.

"On our right" said Pompon, "is the Old New Orleans Court Building." I couldn't believe my luck — to have arrived in such a place! To be greeted by such a dog!

"And on our left, the world-renowned Brennan's Restaurant. And around this corner—"

11

"Ah ha!" cried Pompon. "It's Stella!" And that's how I met another distinguished resident of the French Quarter, Champion Stella de Chateau Blanc.

"Those look like new ribbons you're wearing today, Stella," said Pompon.

"Yes. Best of breed and best of show. Do you like them? Are they straight? Is everybody looking at them?"

Well, everyone *was* looking. Pompon the dancing dog and Champion Stella de Chateau Blanc were an impressive pair. I felt like somebody important just walking in their company.

But I was hungry. As Pompon pointed out the sights of the Quarter and as Stella showed off her ribbons, I peered down an alley at a food dish very much like mine at home.

"Notice, if you will, the ironwork here —" I heard Pompon say as I made my way toward the dish.

"Watch out for the Cat," Stella added.

I bit into the first juicy morsel. The very idea! Watch out for a cat!

Then a shadow fell over me, larger than any cat shadow.

And that is how I met the Catahoula Hound — better known as the Cat.
If I were to describe her growl, her teeth, her eyes, her drool, you might
conclude that I was scared out of my wits. But I was too filled with *admiration*
for the Cat to be afraid of her. Here was the dog I wanted to be!

My story might have ended right here if Pompon and Stella had not come
to my rescue. Fortunately, the Cat was their particular friend, and after proper
introductions the four of us were strolling beneath the galleries of Toulouse Street.

"How do you *do* that?" I asked the Cat. "How do you growl so savagely?
How do you make your eyes glow like coals? How do you curl your lip like a wild
beast?"

"Born that way," said the Cat. She was a dog of few words.

"I was a watchdog once," I confided as we turned down Decatur.

"I'm not a watchdog," said the Cat.

"Attention, please," demanded Pompon.

"Here is Jackson Square!"

We didn't have anything to match this in my old neighborhood. Why, there were clowns and tap dancers and acrobats. There were mimes and minstrels and jugglers. Pompon danced. Champion Stella de Chateau Blanc displayed her ribbons. The Cat plopped down like a junkyard dog ready to guard the whole show.

And I played! I ran races. I chased pigeons and frisbees and mule-drawn carriages. And just when I thought life couldn't offer more — I marched in a parade!

A man took a trumpet out of a suitcase and played a few warm-up notes. I looked up at him. He looked down at me and said, "OK, buddy, let's go!"

He started across the square, playing the notes, pointing his trumpet at the sky, then down to the ground, then to the right, then to the left. At first there were just two of us in the parade, then five, then ten, then more than you could count. But I was always up front leading with the trumpet man.

What a place I had travelled to! What friends I had made!

And then it was time for everyone to go home.

"I'm hungry," said Pompon.

"My coat needs brushing," said Stella.

"Don't go," I began.

But they were gone.

20

Daylight began slipping away. The old gas lights around the square began to glow.

"When the sun goes down," said the Cat, "I go on duty."

"But I thought you said you weren't a watchdog."

"I'm not," she answered. "I'm a guard dog. Different kind of dog. More dangerous line of work. A watchdog like you, well, he just barks."

"Just barks?"

"Yes. At mail carriers and meter readers and next door neighbors. A watchdog may do nothing his whole life but bark at harmless people."

"But then, what's the point in being a watchdog!" I cried.

"The point is," said the Cat, "that your owner depends on you to bark. Because some night there might be—"

"There might be *what*?"

"There might be an intruder." And then the Cat went home, too.

21

Now I was all alone. I walked along the streets. I ate a piece of bread with mustard on it. When it got dark, I climbed up to the levee and lay down. The moon slid from behind the clouds, and I saw a big dog, staring out over the river. Just then he raised his head toward the moon and howled. And from all along the river the answers came rolling back.

"Excuse me," I said to the big dog, "but who are you calling to?"

"I don't know," he said. He didn't even look at me.

"I'm Gumbo," I said. He didn't answer. "I'm glad to find someone who hasn't gone home."

"I don't have a home," he said. "If I did, I'd go there."

While I was thinking of something to say next, the big dog just walked away. He didn't even say goodbye.

I fell asleep thinking about the dog with no home and thinking about my home and wondering if this might be the night an intruder came, with no watchdog there to warn Gus.

The river and I woke up together the next morning. I was really hungry
by then.

I'm glad I got to see those steamboats and cargo ships and barges and
paddle wheelers. Here was a whole new way to travel! If I had got on one of
those, I might have really seen the world!

But I didn't.

I ran the other way — straight back to those streetcar tracks. I just jumped on board! We rolled away from Canal Street, back past the old mansions and the shotgun houses. And then I could see MY NEIGHBORHOOD!

We flew by the postman. "Hey, Gumbo!" he called. "Where have you *been*?"

We flew by the girl in the polka dot dress. "Gumbo!" she cried. "Where've you *been*?"

Then I went right out the streetcar window because I could see MY HOUSE!

And there in front of my house was Gus,
nailing a sign to the old oak tree:

LOST
VALUABLE
WATCHDOG
BIG REWARD!

"Gumbo!" called Gus. "WHERE HAVE YOU BEEN?"
I wished I could tell him I'd been downtown.

I didn't have to tell
him I was home!

The object of our search is present with us.
HORACE

Dear Parents and Educators:

For both children and adults, "running away" sometimes presents itself as a solution to our problems. A gate swings open like an invitation, just as it does for Gumbo, and we see an opportunity to escape. A hallmark of self-esteem is the awareness that there is no geographical cure for life's difficulties, that it is within ourselves that we must find what we seek.

Ideally, home is where, as children, we first learn this lesson and achieve the self-esteem we need to help us face life's adversities. How do our homes help nurture this strong sense of identity and security?

Home is, first of all, a place — our neighborhood, our street, our dwelling. It is a familiar world where we find the familiar physical aspects of our everyday lives. The cracks in the sidewalk, the welcome mat, our father's pot of geraniums, our favorite chair, our books and playthings, the window ledge where we daydream, the very cups from which we drink — all contribute to a comfortable sense of belonging.

Home is also a set of relationships — a family. It is where we know and are known, love and are loved, need and are needed. Home is where nothing is more important than this give and take with others.

Home is also, as Gumbo discovers, a place we make for ourselves, that we achieve for ourselves through the fulfillment of our responsibilities and the performance of acts of thoughtfulness, consideration, and caring.

Few homes consistently live up to this ideal. Some fall far short. But underlying Gumbo's story is an encouraging message: through our own efforts, building on what we have, we can hope to find contentment right where we are.

Here are some questions you might ask to help children think about the message of *Gumbo Goes Downtown*:

- How does Gus show that he cares about Gumbo?
- Why does Gumbo feel like a big nobody?
- Why does Gumbo decide to run away?
- What are the special talents of Pompon, Stella, and the Cat?
- How is Gumbo special?
- Why do you think Gumbo decides to go back home?

Here are some things you can do to help children appreciate their homes and their own importance in their homes:

- Explore the many varieties of homes and families.
- Encourage recognition of specific ways family members depend upon one another.
- Help children identify their unique contributions to the functioning of their households.
- As parents, provide children opportunities to fulfill clearly defined responsibilities to the home and family.

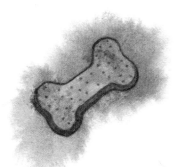

Available from MarshMedia

These storybooks, each hardcover with dustjacket and full-color illustrations throughout, are available at bookstores, or you may order at marshmedia.com or by calling toll free: 800-821-3303.

Aloha Potter! written by Linda Talley, illustrated by Andra Chase, 32 pages.

Amazing Mallika, written by Jami Parkison, illustrated by Itoko Maeno, 32 pages.

Bailey's Birthday, written by Elizabeth Happy, illustrated by Andra Chase, 32 pages.

Bastet, written by Linda Talley, illustrated by Itoko Maeno, 32 pages.

Bea's Own Good, written by Linda Talley, illustrated by Andra Chase, 32 pages.

Clarissa, written by Carol Talley, illustrated by Itoko Maeno, 32 pages.

Dream Catchers, written by Lisa Suhay, illustrated by Louis S. Glanzman, 40 pages.

Emily Breaks Free, written by Linda Talley, illustrated by Andra Chase, 32 pages.

Feathers at Las Flores, written by Linda Talley, illustrated by Andra Chase, 32 pages.

Following Isabella, written by Linda Talley, illustrated by Andra Chase, 32 pages.

Gumbo Goes Downtown, written by Carol Talley, illustrated by Itoko Maeno, 32 pages.

Hana's Year, written by Carol Talley, illustrated by Itoko Maeno, 32 pages.

Inger's Promise, written by Jami Parkison, illustrated by Andra Chase, 32 pages.

Jackson's Plan, written by Linda Talley, illustrated by Andra Chase, 32 pages.

Jomo and Mata, written by Alyssa Chase, illustrated by Andra Chase, 32 pages.

Kiki and the Cuckoo, written by Elizabeth Happy, illustrated by Andra Chase, 32 pages.

Kylie's Concert, written by Patty Sheehan, illustrated by Itoko Maeno, 32 pages.

Kylie's Song, written by Patty Sheehan, illustrated by Itoko Maeno, 32 pages. (Paper Posie, LLC)

Ludmila's Way, written by Linda Talley, illustrated by Andra Chase, 32 pages.

Minou, written by Mindy Bingham, illustrated by Itoko Maeno, 64 pages. (Paper Posie LLC)

Molly's Magic, written by Penelope Colville Paine, illustrated by Itoko Maeno, 32 pages.

My Way Sally, written by Mindy Bingham and Penelope Paine, illustrated by Itoko Maeno, 48 pages. (Paper Posie, LLC)

Papa Piccolo, written by Carol Talley, illustrated by Itoko Maeno, 32 pages.

Pequeña the Burro, written by Jami Parkison, illustrated by Itoko Maeno, 32 pages.

Plato's Journey, written by Linda Talley, illustrated by Itoko Maeno, 32 pages.

Stanley's "This is the Life!", written by Alyssa Chase Rebein, illustrated by Andra Chase, 32 pages.

Tessa on Her Own, written by Alyssa Chase, illustrated by Itoko Maeno, 32 pages.

Thank You, Meiling, written by Linda Talley, illustrated by Itoko Maeno, 32 pages.

Time for Horatio, written by Penelope Paine, illustrated by Itoko Maeno, 48 pages. (Paper Posie, LLC)

Toad in Town, written by Linda Talley, illustrated by Itoko Maeno, 32 pages.

Tonia the Tree, written by Sandy Stryker, illustrated by Itoko Maeno, 32 pages. (Paper Posie, LLC)

These books are also available in companion Mulitmedia Kits for classroom use. Each kit includes the research-based Evaluation Guide, DVD or video (English or Spanish), Home Ties and 36-page Teaching Guide with reproducible worksheets. MarshMedia has been publishing award-winning learning materials for children since 1969. To order or to recieve a free catalog, call 800-821-3303, or visit us at marshmedia.com